For Jake. Best friend, best dog. — A.S.
For Tegan, who really can. — L.M.

ISBN-13: 978-0-545-06164-3

ISBN-10: 0-545-06164-4

Text copyright © 2008 by Amber Stewart

Illustrations copyright © 2008 by Layn Marlow

All rights reserved. First published in Great Britain by Oxford University Press in 2008.

Cover illustration © 2008 by Layn Marlow

First Scholastic printing, January 2008

Amber Stewart & Layn Marlow

Little by Little

Orchard Books / New York

an imprint of Scholastic Inc.

Otto was making a list.
An I CAN DO list and an
I CAN'T DO list.

The CAN DO side was much longer.
On it was:

Forward roly-poly

Backward roly-poly

Being kind to frogs

Mud sliding

Making very good
sand castles

Slippery-rock
hopping.

The CAN'T DO side was shorter.
It just said . . .

swimming.

"Otto, are you going to
swim today?" asked Beaver.

"No," said Otto.

"Not at all?" asked Bear. "Not even a little?"

Otto sighed and went home.

"Don't listen to Bear and Beaver," said
his mommy, when Otto told her.
"Little by little, you will learn to swim."

Otto decided he would have to keep trying.

Sometimes, Otto would
pretend he could swim,
but really he was hopping —
very, very quickly —
along the riverbed.

Other times, he would run along
the riverbank, trying not to be
left behind by his friends as
they spun and tumbled
through the water.

But most days, Otto would simply sit on
his favorite slippery rock — wishing and wishing
from his whiskers all the way down to his toes —
that he could swim.

Every day, his mommy
would say, "Today's the day."

And every day — it wasn't.

Then, one sunny day, Otto and his sister were watching their friends jumping off the Highest-Ever Rock into the Deepest-Ever Pool below.
"You have got to start small," his sister said.
"Small?" said Otto.

"Yes, small," she said. "Come on.
Today is the day to start small.
That's how I did it when
I learned to swim."

So, Otto started small. He hopped along the riverbed, keeping his toes off the bottom just that little bit longer every time.

Then, he did higher hops,
with floating in between.

The next day, Otto did floating without
holding on to anything,

and pretty soon, he was kicking all the way
to the Halfway Stone.

A few days later, Otto splashed and
kicked and swam the whole width
of the river — from one bank to
the other — all by himself.

And little by little, that width became
the length of the river from Otto's den
to the Deepest-Ever Pool.

Before long, the splashing and kicking
turned into gliding, and roly-polies
on the riverbank became
underwater tumbling.

When he was ready, Otto
invited his friends and
family to come see his
big surprise. With everyone
gathered along the
riverbank . . .

Otto jumped off the
Highest-Ever Rock into the
Deepest-Ever Pool.

"I did it," said Otto to his sister.
"I can really swim!"

"You really can," laughed his sister, hugging her very wet little brother.

"You see. You started small . . . and finished big!"